VISIT OUR STORE
at
1600 Highway 6, Ste. 480
Sugar Land, TX 77478

**Swami Dayanand
Educational Foundation**
1600 Highway 6, Ste. 480
Sugar Land, TX 77478

Subhas Chandra Bose

Netaji

imprint of Om Books International

Published in 2014 by

An imprint of Om Books International

Corporate & Editorial Office
A 12, Sector 64, Noida 201 301
Uttar Pradesh, India
Phone: +91 120 477 4100
Email: editorial@ombooks.com
Website: www.ombooksinternational.com

Sales Office
4379/4B, Prakash House, Ansari Road
Darya Ganj, New Delhi 110 002, India
Phone: +91 11 2326 3363, 2326 5303
Fax: +91 11 2327 8091
Email: sales@ombooks.com
Website: www.ombooks.com

Written by Subhojit Sanyal
Illustrations: Braj Kishore, Jyoti Pawar, Naushad

ISBN : 978-93-80069-97-5

Printed at EIH Press, Gurgaon, India

10 9 8 7 6 5 4 3 2 1

Contents

Birth and Childhood

There was reason for great joy and celebration in the household of the renowned lawyer, Janaki Nath Bose in Cuttack, then a part of the Bengal Presidency. It was the 23 January 1897 and his wife, Prabhavati had given birth to their ninth child Subhas Chandra Bose. They had fourteen children in all.

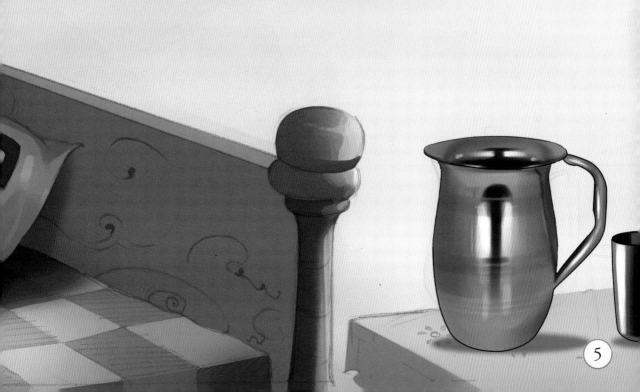

Subhas Bose began his early schooling at the Anglo School in Cuttack, which was later renamed as Stewart School.

Subhas Bose was a bright student and this was evident to his teachers right from the very start.

However, the Anglo School in Cuttack at that time only functioned till the seventh standard therefore Subhas Bose had to transfer to the Ravenshaw Collegiate School to continue his studies.

This was around the same time that Bangla was made a compulsory subject for Bengalis at the matriculation level. Subhas Bose was very happy with the change as the Anglo School did not teach Bangla as a subject.

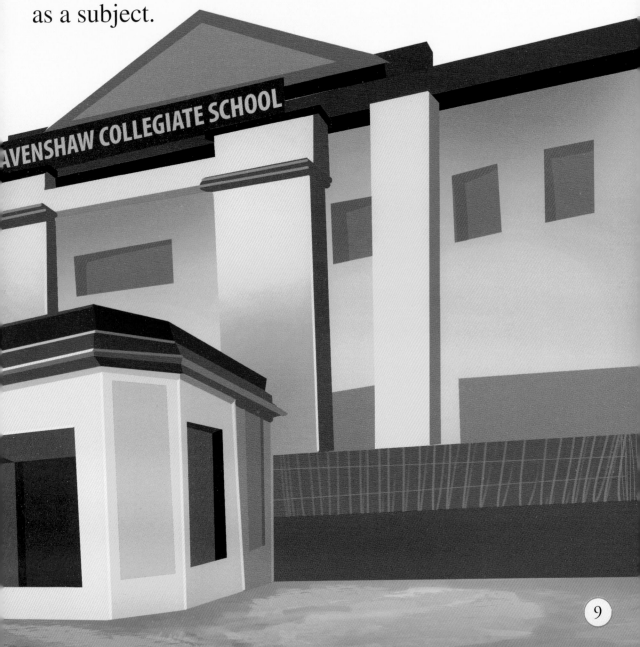

Emergence of Nationalistic Sentiments

At the Ravenshaw Collegiate School under the leadership of the principal Beni Madhav Das, Subhas Bose started understanding the concept of freedom and developed love for his country. While the Anglo School had a western uniform, the students at Ravenshaw Collegiate wore kurtas and dhotis as uniform. Subhas Bose proudly wore his new uniform to school.

By the time he turned fifteen, Subhas Bose voraciously started reading the works of Swami Vivekananda and was extremely impressed with the great sage's writings. He stood second in his matriculation exams. Subhas Bose decided to spend some time in search for a spiritual guru by visiting various holy places, before he joined college.

However, the materialistic values of the sages he met disillusioned him. Realising that he would have to pursue his goals and ideals without a spiritual guide, Subhas Bose started attending college at the prestigious Presidency College in Calcutta (now called Kolkata).

"...If this belief from heaven be sent, If such be Nature's holy plan, Have I not reason to lament What man has made of man?"

- William Wordsworth

14

In college, he noticed that the English professors spoke in an extremely derogatory manner with the Indian students. However, it was Professor Oaten's remarks about Indians being savages and the British being their educators that filled Subhas Bose with rage. Leading a team of Indian students, Subhas Bose appealed to the principal Professor James to ask Professor Oaten to apologise for his comments. However, the Principal himself being an Englishman, refused.

The enraged Subhas Bose called for a strike at the college. More than a thousand students participated in it, classes could not be held and even the Indian teachers supported it. Finally after three days, Professor Oaten issued a public apology for his comments.

Christina Rossetti (1830 - 1894)
was a gifted poet.

Disillusionment with Peaceful Protests

Once college resumed after the strike, Professor Oaten continued to humiliate the students to take revenge for the embarrassment he had to suffer.

One evening, just as Professor Oaten was about to leave the college, a group of boys attacked him, injuring him severely.

Subhas Bose was summoned to the Principal's Office at once.

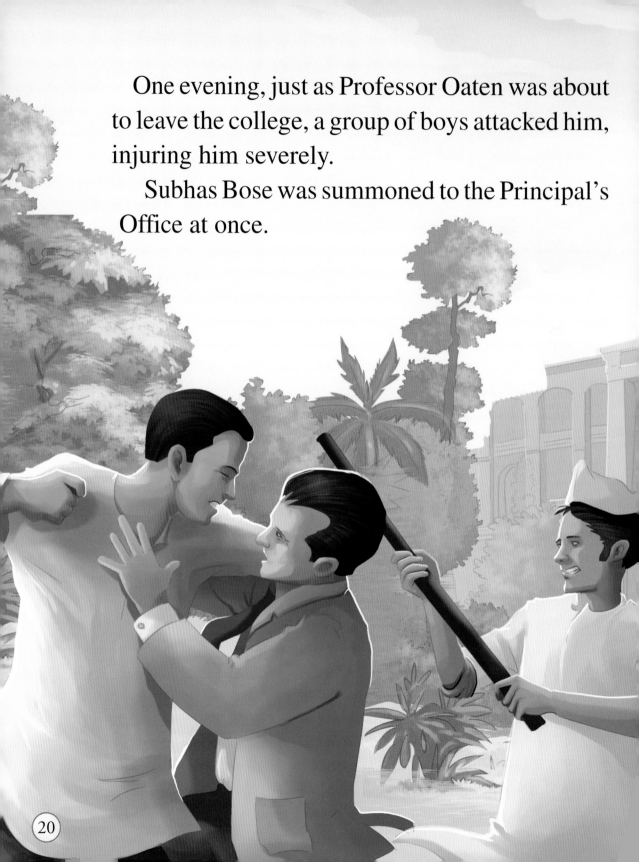

Principal James declared that the authorities had enough reason to believe that Subhas Bose too was part of the attack and therefore was expelled from college.

Subhas Bose returned to Cuttack and started working for the betterment of the poor people there. As his fame grew in the region, Sir Ashutosh Mukherjee, Vice Chancellor of Calcutta University, was able to help him secure admission in Scottish Church College. During this time Subhas Bose joined the University Training Corps. It was here that he first realised that an armed resistance against the British would perhaps be more effective in attaining independence for the country. Subhas Bose soon turned out to be one of the best soldiers at the Corps.

Agitating against Oppression

After Subhas Bose graduated from Calcutta University, he travelled to England and secured admission in Fitzwilliam College, University of Cambridge in 1919. He was fulfilling his father's dreams by sitting for the Indian Civil Services examination, which was held in England at that time. The results were declared: Subhas Bose stood fourth in the examinations.

However, now that he had fulfilled his father's wishes and cleared the ICS examinations with merit, Subhas Bose resigned from the services.

He wrote a letter to the British Secretary of State for India, E.S. Montagu and made it clear that he had no intentions of serving a foreign government and instead decided to work actively towards the freedom his country.

Armed Resistance
v/s Non-violence

The first thing that Subhas Bose did on arriving in India was meet Mahatma Gandhi in July 1921. Gandhi explained to Subhas Bose that his methods for achieving freedom were completely non-violent. Subhas Bose agreed that ahimsa as a tool for achieving freedom was good in principle, but he insisted that an armed resistance was better. Seeing Subhas Bose's passion, Gandhi suggested that was Subhas Bose start work under "Deshbandhu" Chittaranjan Das's guidance.

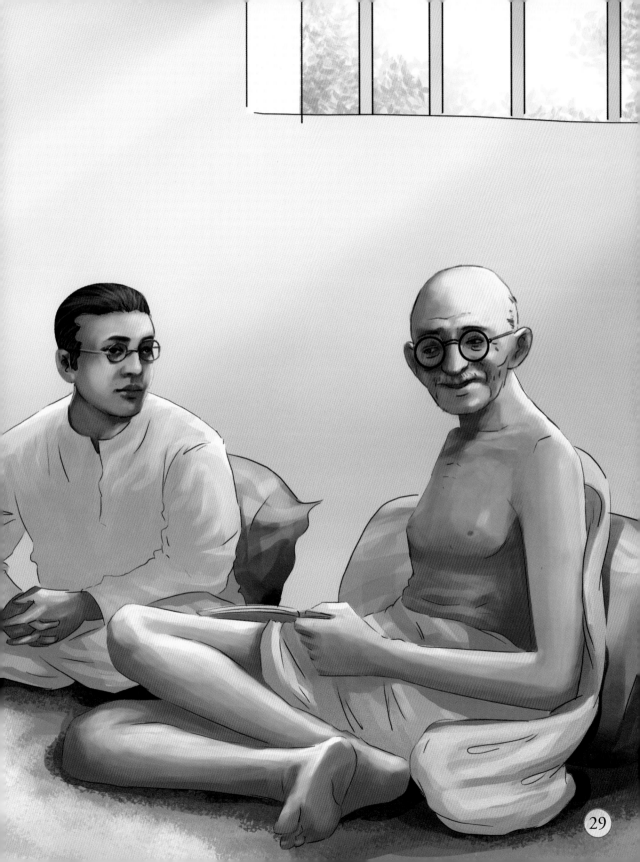

Chittaranjan Das, a member of the Congress Party, was one of the biggest political leaders at that time. He warmly received Subhas Bose and Bose knew at once that he had found his guru.

During this time, Subhas Bose also founded the newspaper, *Swaraj*, and took over responsibility for the publicity of the Bengal Provincial Congress Committee. Bose was elected as the President of the All India Youth Congress in 1923 and he also served as the Secretary to the Bengal State Congress.

The Swaraj Party

Chittaranjan Das soon formed his own party the Swaraj Party. In 1924, the Swaraj Party won the Calcutta Corporation Elections.

Chittaranjan Das became the new Mayor of Calcutta and Subhas Bose the CEO of the Calcutta Corporation. Under the leadership of Chittaranjan Das and Subhas Bose, the Swaraj Party contributed greatly to the city.

They made several changes to the Corporation and the most important one was making khadi the official dress code of all the workers there.

Subhas Bose formed Volunteer Corps which sold Swadeshi goods at reasonable prices to the people and also carry out other social and political tasks. However, this upset the British Government, who declared the Volunteer Corps to be illegal.

Subhas Bose refused to give in and members of the Volunteer Corps openly started protesting against the order.

Coincidentally, the tensions in the city rose to a crescendo when a European was found murdered in the city. Subhas Bose was held responsible for the murder and arrested.

Imprisoned at the Mandalay Jail in Burma

People started protesting outside the Presidency Jail in Calcutta where Subhas Bose was imprisoned. Fearing a public backlash against Subhas Bose's arrest, the British moved him to the Mandalay Jail in Burma.

The inhuman conditions soon had a negative impact on Subhas Bose's health. In a few days' time, he contracted tuberculosis.

Subhas Bose's condition grew from bad to worse and no sooner did the news of his failing health reach Calcutta, the nation erupted in a mad frenzy. People demanded that he be released immediately.

The British Government tried to make a deal with Subhas Bose that he would be granted his freedom, provided he left for Europe immediately.

Subhas Bose made it very clear to his captors that he would only accept an unconditional release from prison or else he would prefer to die in jail. On seeing his condition worsen, Subhas Bose was granted an unconditional release and allowed to return to India in 1927.

Subhas Bose spent the next few months at Dalhousie, recuperating from tuberculosis. During this time, he learnt that Chittaranjan Das had passed away during his absence. Subhas Bose was very sad and resolved to make his mentor's dreams come true one day.

Becoming Mayor of Calcutta

Subhas Bose organised a Volunteer Corps using Congress supporters to continue their agitation in a unified manner.

Naturally, the British did not take this lightly and Subhas Bose was arrested for civil disobedience.

In 1930, while Subhas Bose was still in jail, he was elected as the Mayor of Calcutta. The British Government was forced to release him so that he could take up his duties in his new elected office.

Subhas Bose continued leading civil disobedience movements against the British even as he dispensed his duties as the Mayor.

Imprisoned Yet Again

As Subhas Bose continued to agitate against the Britishers, they arrested him again. Owing to the poor condition of the cell he was kept in, Subhas Bose fell ill once again.

Back at home, the appeals for his release were increasing and Bose was once again released by the British, fearing a public backlash that could get out of hand. But the Britishers released him only on one condition: he had to leave India and go to Europe.

Appealing to the World

Subhas used his time in exile to travel to various countries and appeal to the world against British atrocities in India. Around this time he secretly married the Austrian Emilie Schenki.

Owing to the increase in his popularity as a leader, Subhas Bose was nominated as the Congress President in the 1938 Haripura session. As the Congress President, Subhas Bose was very vocal that India needs to fight the British in armed combat. He was convinced that there would perhaps never be a better time for Indians to fight the British.

Gandhi's Opposition

Subhas Bose's call for armed revolution was having a clear impact on the Congress leadership, most of whom were under the aegis of Gandhi. Gandhi was

against Subhas Bose's candidature for the next term and he endorsed Pattabhi Sitaramayya for the post of Congress President at the Tripura session in 1939.

Subhas Bose won even though Gandhi opposed him! This made one thing very clear in Subhas Bose's mind—the country was now ready to fight against the British.

Sadly, Subhas Bose also realised that his disagreement with Gandhi's non-violence methods would have a detrimental impact on the Congress. He was falling into dispute with Jawaharlal Nehru over the methods for independence, and soon he resigned from the Congress Party. In May 1939, Subhas Bose formed the All India Forward Bloc party.

The first major movement of the Forward Bloc was to protest against Viceroy Lord Linlithgow's decision to include India against the war on Hitler. Subhas Bose led his supporters to the Holwell Monument, which was erected by the British to act as an edict about the slavery of Indians to the British.

This act of civil disobedience led to Subhas Bose's arrest. He was imprisoned in the Presidency Jail again.

Subhas Bose went on a hunger strike for seven days which forced the British to release him. He was however kept on house arrest.

Travelling the World in Disguise

Subhas Bose knew that he would not be able to do anything for his country by being imprisoned at home. He therefore hatched a plan to escape.

On the night of 19 January 1941, Sisir Kumar Bose drove his uncle Subhas Bose who had concealed himself at the back of the car to the station. Subhas Bose, disguised as an insurance agent, was soon aboard the train going to Peshawar.

Subhas Bose finally travelled to Moscow via the North-West Frontier Province (NWFP) and Afghanistan to seek Soviet help in India's battle against the British. As he couldn't speak even a syllable of Pashto, the local language, Subhas Bose pretended to be a deaf and dumb Pathan.

Subhas Bose and his guide, Bhagat Ram Talwar, reached Kabul as stowaways in a lorry. However, on reaching Kabul, they learnt that Germany had invaded the USSR, and therefore, the Soviets were now allies with the British. Subhas Bose hence decided to seek help from the Italians and Germans. Disguised as an Italian nobleman, Subhas Bose reached Berlin where he made his true identity public once again.

Leading Operations from Berlin

Subhas Bose used Berlin as his centre of operations. He made several speeches against the British rule in India on the German-sponsored Azad Hind Radio.

Finally Subhas Bose met Hitler, requesting him to offer assistance in fighting the British forces in India. By the end of July 1942, with Nazi assistance, Subhas Bose was able to etablish the Free India Legion, an Army division consisting of soldiers who were captured by the Germans as prisoners of wars against the British forces in northern Africa.

However, Subhas Bose soon realised that the now-retreating German army can no longer be a constructive partner against the British forces in India. He therefore sought the help of the Japanese.

Becoming Netaji

In February 1943, Subhas Bose set sail towards the South East Asia. As he was nearing Tokyo, Subhas Bose transferred to a Japanese submarine, in which he arrived at Tokyo. He was quickly taken to Singapore, where he was welcomed by Indian revolutionaries like Rash Behari Bose.

It was here that Subhas Bose formed the bulk of his army, the Indian National Army (INA), with the Indian prisoners of war, who had been taken captive by the Japanese while they were fighting for the British. Subhas Bose also formed the Rani of Jhansi regiment, which was made up only of women soldiers. This was also the same time around when the soldiers of the INA started calling him "Netaji" out of respect.

Indian National Army

Netaji finally announced the formation of the Azad Hind Fauz (Indian National Army) in October 1943. The INA was ready to fight the British to reclaim their motherland. "Delhi Chalo" was the war cry of the army.

As the INA started its march towards India, Subhas Bose gave the war cry, "Give me blood and I will give you freedom!" Many Indians came out in great support of the INA, most of them donating generously towards its cost of operations.

In March 1944 the British Forces along the Assam border were surprised by a sudden INA strike. The British forces were routed in no time.

The INA continued their march towards Kohima, which soon fell to the INA forces and the Indian national flag was hoisted there to declare the INA's victory.

However, the British were successful in sending sufficient reinforcements to Imphal and the INA's hold started to fall. To make matters worse, the Allied offensive on Japan had increased manifold and the Japanese were no longer able to support the INA with sufficient food and supplies. The INA was stranded!

To make matters even worse for the INA, the monsoons started at the same time, causing the outbreak of several diseases and illness amongst the troops. However, Netaji was still not ready to give up. He called on them to refuel their spirits and continue in their fight against the British.

Netaji established that dying while fighting was still a better option than accepting defeat.

Netaji's Mysterious Disappearance

The conditions on the ground were deteriorating by the minute. The Japanese forces had surrendered to the US–British forces who were now hunting for Netaji. There was a serious threat to Netaji's life as the British did not want to take any more chances with him.

The INA soldiers were able to convince Netaji to escape and begin another movement from another nation.

Finally on 17 August 1945, Netaji boarded a plane along with Colonel Habibur Rahman for an unknown location though it is believed that the plane was heading for Tokyo from where Netaji planned to escape to Moscow. However, that plane was never found and Netaji was never seen by anyone again. There have been many theories about his sudden disappearance.

Many historians are of the opinion that the Japanese aircraft carrying Bose crashed and that Netaji died a few hours later. It is also believed that his ashes are kept at the Renkoji Temple in Tokyo. However, some studies also point to the fact that the ashes kept at the temple do not belong to Netaji. Moreover, American satellite pictures and documents insist that no plane crashed in Taipei region that day.

Many other historians believe that Netaji might have been arrested en route to Moscow by the Soviets and imprisoned till his death in Siberia.

As Netaji's body was never found, many people believed that Netaji may still be alive, and there were claims that a mysterious sadhu had arrived in Banaras after India attained independence, who had confessed to a few trusted associates that he was Subhas Bose.

The Unsung Hero

No one will ever know the truth about Netaji's disappearance after that fateful flight in August 1945, but one truth will always remain—Netaji Subhas Chandra Bose was one of the most glorious sons of the country, who fought with unwavering passion and vigour for his motherland.

TITLES IN THIS SERIES

     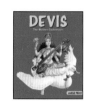

   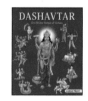  

 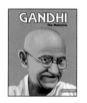  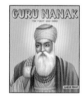